Pokémon

READER

LET IT SNOW!

Adapted by Tracey West

Scholastic Inc.

New York   Toronto   London   Auckland   Sydney
Mexico City   New Delhi   Hong Kong   Buenos Aires

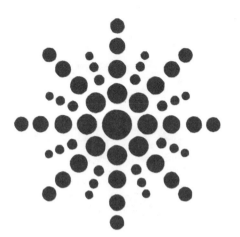

ISBN 0-439-42989-7

12 11 10 9 8 7 6 5 4 3   3 4 5 6 7/0

Printed in the U.S.A.
First printing, December 2002

Team Rocket was climbing Snow Top
Peak, too.

But Team Rocket was in trouble. They
were stuck on a ledge.

"We are going to freeze!" wailed
Jessie.

A Pokémon flew down from the sky. Snow fell all around it.

"What is that?" cried Meowth.

The Pokémon took Team Rocket to a safe place.

Ash and his friends climbed up Snow Top Peak. They did not know Team Rocket was nearby.

Soon they came to a Pokémon Center. Officer Jenny was there, too.

Todd could not wait to find Articuno.

"I want to take a picture of it," Todd told Officer Jenny.

"Articuno is a rare Pokémon," said Jenny. "Not many people have seen one."

Nurse Joy heard them talking.

"You have come to the right place," she said. "Articuno lives on Snow Top Peak. It helps people who are in trouble."

Nurse Joy and Officer Jenny led them all outside.

"An Articuno statue!" said Ash. "That is cool."

Just then, a wind began to blow. Snow
began to fall.

Then the wind and snow stopped.

"It's Team Rocket!" Ash cried.
Jessie, James, and Meowth had fallen to
the ground with the snow.

Team Rocket told their story.

"Articuno must have helped them,"
Todd said. "Just like Nurse Joy told us."

Todd wanted to go find Articuno right away. Ash and his friends ran after him. They all climbed up the peak. Jigglypuff followed them.

"Oh no!" Misty cried. "It is snowing again!"

The snow fell harder and harder. The friends could not see anything but white snow.

"*Pika! Pika!*" said Pikachu.

"What is it, Pikachu?" Ash asked.

All of a sudden, a Pokémon flew right in front of them.

"Articuno!" Todd cried.

The friends stopped and stared at the beautiful Pokémon.

Ash took a step closer. Articuno cried
out. Then Ash looked down.

They were about to walk off a cliff!
They could not see their way because
of the snow. Articuno had saved them.

Todd tried to take a picture of Articuno.
But something attacked the Pokémon!

It was Team Rocket!

"Why are you doing this?" Ash asked them. "Articuno helped you."

"Now Articuno can help us again," said James. "It can let us bring it back to the Boss!"

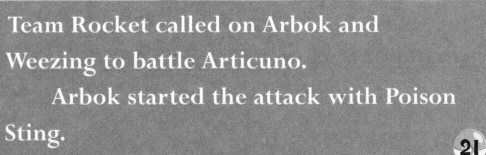

Team Rocket called on Arbok and
Weezing to battle Articuno.
    Arbok started the attack with Poison
Sting.

The Poison Sting did not hurt Articuno.
It fought back with Ice Beam.

Jessie called on Wobbuffet. Wobbuffet used a move called Mirror Coat. It sent the Ice Beam right back at Articuno.

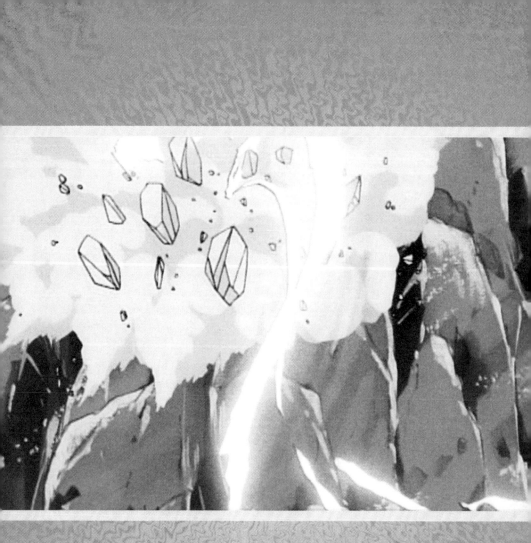

Articuno moved just in time. The Ice Beam hit the snowy peak. Big chunks of ice broke off.

The falling ice broke the cliff! Ash
and Todd went tumbling down.

"*Pika!*" cried Pikachu. It jumped
off the cliff to help Ash.
Jigglypuff jumped off, too.

Jigglypuff puffed up. It floated to the
ground with Pikachu on its back. They
found Ash and Todd.

"Hey, we are not hurt," Ash said.

Then Team Rocket came crashing down. They did not want to give up.

Arbok attacked Articuno with Poison Sting.

Weezing attacked Articuno with Sludge.

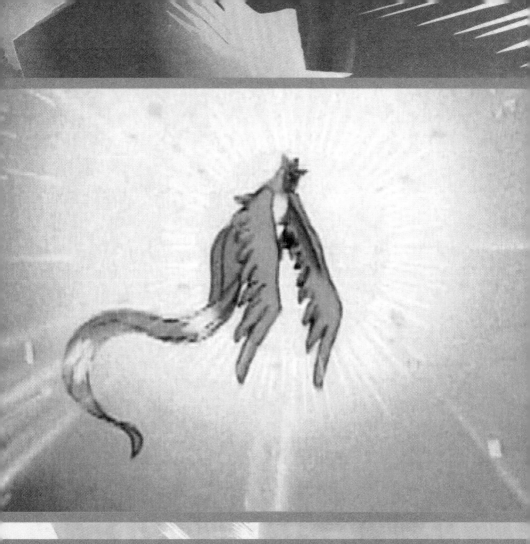

Articuno used Blizzard.

Cold snow fell from the sky. A strong wind hit Team Rocket.

"We are blasting off again!" they yelled. Then the wind took Team Rocket far, far away.

The sun came out. Articuno twinkled in the golden light.

Todd took a picture.
"That is just the picture I wanted," he said with a smile.

Brock and Misty rode up in a
snowmobile.

"Are you all right?" Misty asked.

"We sure are," Ash said. "Thanks to
Articuno!"

"*Pikachu!*" said Pikachu.